The Donkey Prince

The Donkey Prince

adapted from Grimm by

M. JEAN CRAIG

illustrated by

BARBARA COONEY

BARNES
&NOBLE
BOOKS
NEW YORK

This edition published by Barnes & Noble, Inc.,
by arrangement with Bantam Doubleday Dell,
a division of Random House

1999 Barnes & Noble Books

ISBN 0-7607-0695-6

Printed in Spain by Gráficas Estella, S.A.

99 00 01 02 03 04 MC 9 8 7 6 5 4 3 2 1

Once there lived a King and a Queen who ruled over a wide and peaceful kingdom.

The King loved nothing better than his riches. He spent most of his time in his strongroom, counting silver bars and golden coins and bags of rubies and pearls.

The Queen loved nothing better than pretty clothes. She spent most of her time before her mirror, trying on gowns and robes, collars and capes, feathers and silks and furs.

The King and the Queen were really quite happy. They would have been very happy, except for one thing. They had no children.

"If only we had a child!" the Queen would say. "If only we had a little girl with long hair, and then I could dress her up in laces and bows!"

"If only we had a son!" the King would say. "If only we had a handsome, bright lad who looked just like me!"

There was a nursery in the castle, full of playthings to please a little girl with long hair or a handsome little boy. But there were spiderwebs on the dolls and the hoop, and dust covered the balls and the hobbyhorse, because there was no one there to use them.

Then one day a traveler came to the castle and spoke of a Wizard who lived deep in the Great Forest.

"He is a very powerful Wizard," said the traveler. "He has magic spells for anything that anyone might want."

"I already have all the gold and silver and jewels that I want," said the King. "Or almost all."

"I already have all the dresses and hats and ribbons that I want," said the Queen. "Or almost all."

"But we do not have a child," said the King.

"And we do want a child," said the Queen.

"Do you think the Wizard has a magic spell to help us have a child?" the King asked the traveler.

"Oh, I am certain of it," said the traveler. "He is a very powerful Wizard."

So the King and the Queen rode their horses into the Great Forest to the cave where the Wizard lived.

"A spell to help you have a child? Of course I have one," said the Wizard. "I have a magic spell for anything that anyone might want. But you must pay me, of course, before I use it."

"Of course, of course," said the King.

"You must pay me," the Wizard went on, "thirty-three bags of gold coins."

"Thirty-three *bags*!" shouted the King. "Thirty-three *full* bags?"

"Yes, thirty-three full bags," said the Wizard, "and a baby will be born to you before the violets bloom."

As the King and Queen rode home through the Great Forest, the Queen thought about having the nursery dusted and swept. But the King thought about the thirty-three *full* bags of coins he had promised to send to the Wizard.

In his strongroom, the King sadly began to fill the bags. But then he remembered something. Under a shelf was an old box full of lead pieces which had been dipped in gold paint. The King pulled it out and opened it.

"These look just like real gold," the King said to himself, and he smiled. "I will slip a handful of them into the bottom of each bag, and the Wizard will never know the difference."

But when the King's men delivered the bags to the Wizard, the Wizard sniffed them, one at a time, and his face turned purple with rage.

"Lead!" cried the Wizard. "I smell lead in every bag! No one ever cheats the Wizard!"

Then he lit a magic fire and said some magic words and cast his magic spell.

"The King and the Queen shall have their child," he cackled, as he danced around the magic flames. "Oh yes! They shall have their child! But it will be shaped like a donkey! And it will look like a donkey all its life, unless someone can forget its shape and love it as a human being is loved!" And the Wizard danced and cackled until the magic fire went out.

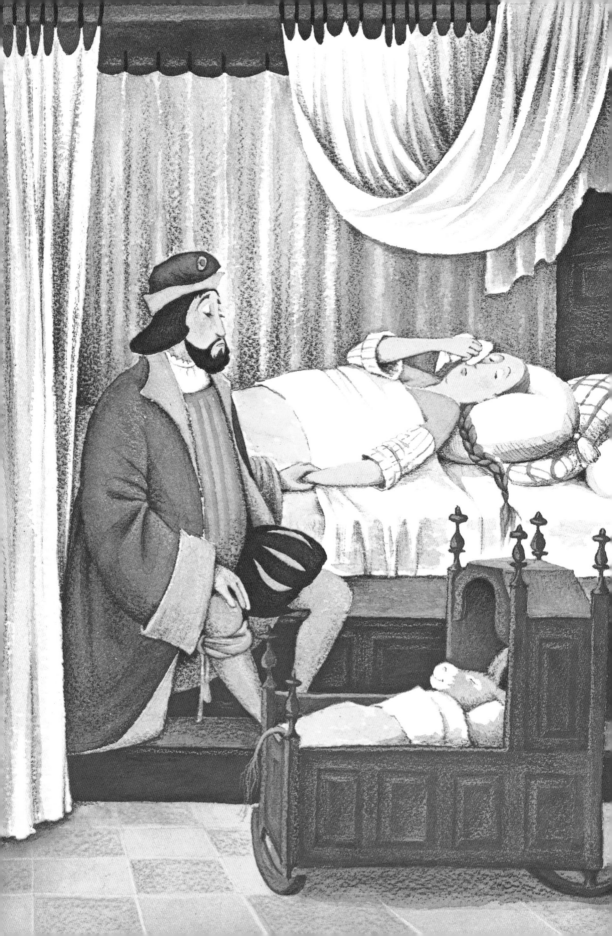

Early in the spring, a child was born to the King and the Queen. But there was no joy in the castle.

"That gray fur!" the Queen wept. "Those dreadful, dreadful ears!"

"That long tail!" the King moaned. "That tail with a tassel on the end!"

"It is the Wizard's fault!" cried the Queen. "He must be punished!"

"No," the King said sadly. "He knew I tried to cheat him. This is how he has punished us."

"But what shall we do with this—this *donkey*?"

"Whatever his shape, he is still the child of the King and the Queen," said the King. "It is our duty to bring him up as a prince."

And so the little donkey was treated like any other baby prince. He was dressed in little jackets and caps. As he grew, he learned to speak, and to sit nicely in a chair, and to eat neatly. When he was older, he was taught how to add and to spell, and also how to dance and to play chess and to behave the way a young prince ought to behave.

And he did behave like a young prince.

He always spoke politely to the ladies and gentlemen of the court. But all they said was, "He has rather good manners, hasn't he—for a donkey!"

He worked hard and well at his lessons. But his teachers said only, "For a donkey, he's really quite smart."

He could kick a ball as straight as an arrow, and was very good at races. But the other children who lived at the court would not play with him. They laughed and shouted "Hee-haw! Hee-haw!" and ran away.

And the Donkey Prince almost never saw his mother or his father.

The King did not like to look at him, and spent more time than ever in his strongroom, counting his riches.

The Queen could not bear to look at him, and spent more time than ever in front of her mirror, admiring her pretty clothes.

So, all through the years while he was growing up, the Donkey Prince was a very lonely young prince indeed.

One day a wandering lute player came to the castle to entertain the people of the court. When he had finished playing, the Donkey Prince went to him. "Will you teach me how to play the lute too?" he asked.

The lute player looked at the Donkey Prince's front hoofs. "I really do not think you would be able to manage the strings," he said, but he agreed to try.

At first the Donkey Prince's hoofs did keep tangling in the lute strings. But after a while the lessons went better. The Donkey Prince learned to play all the songs the lute player knew, and then he made up new songs and learned to play them too.

Finally the day came when the lute player said, "There is nothing more that I can teach you. You play better than I do now!"

After the lute player left the castle, the Donkey Prince made up a very special new song. Then he went to find his mother.

The Queen was in her chamber, trying on a white silk robe. The Donkey Prince played his new song to her. It was a soft, loving song. When he had finished, the Queen smoothed down the front of her robe. She did not look at the Donkey Prince.

"Yes, yes," the Queen said. "That is a clever trick you have learned. But I am busy now."

Then the Donkey Prince went to find his father. The King was in the strongroom, counting a stack of shiny silver bars. The Donkey Prince played his new song to the King, softly and lovingly. When he had finished, the King put three more silver bars on the stack. He did not look at the Donkey Prince.

"Yes, yes," said the King. "That is rather pretty. But do go away now. You can see that I am busy."

The Donkey Prince did go away. He went to his own room, and stood before the mirror for a long time. Then he spoke to the donkey-image in the glass.

"I have learned the things that a prince should know," he said, "and I feel like a prince inside. But even when I behave just like any other prince, my mother and father see only these awful ears, and this terrible tail with the tassel on the end."

Tears came to his eyes.

"I am tired of being The-Prince-Who-Is-Only-a-Donkey! I am tired of wearing these foolish clothes, too!" he cried. "I will go away, far away, where I will not *have* to be The-Prince-Who-Is-Only-a-Donkey ever again."

And the Donkey Prince pulled off his velvet coat and breeches and his shirt, and he hung his lute from his neck by its long ribbon, and he left his room, and the castle, and his own land.

For a long time, the Donkey Prince wandered here and there across the countryside. He saw no human faces; he heard no human voice.

Instead, he listened to the wind blowing on the mountaintops, and in the valleys, and learned to

play the many songs of the wind on his lute. He turned the cool, running sound of a shaded brook into music; he heard the song the new moon sings, and played it back, on his lute, into the night, to make the small stars dance in the sky.

Many months passed. Then one morning the Donkey Prince came to a tall castle.

"Good day to you," said the Donkey Prince to the guard standing at the castle gate. "I should like to pay my compliments to the King."

The guard laughed. "*You? You* wish to call on the King? Impossible!"

The Donkey Prince did not answer. Instead, he began to play a lonesome, disappointed tune on his lute.

"My goodness!" said the guard. "How well you play! I'd better tell the King about this."

The King had just sat down to lunch with his daughter, the Princess.

"Excuse me, sire," said the guard, "but there is a donkey at the castle gate who can speak. And he is playing the lute like an angel."

"Well, bring him in," said the King, "so he can play for us."

The Donkey Prince was brought into the dining hall. He bowed to the King and to the Princess, and wished them a good day. Then he began to play his lute.

He played a song about smooth roads winding over green hills to the farthest, farthest edge of the world. The King and the Princess stopped eating.

When the song came to an end, the Princess said, "I have never heard anything so lovely in all my life!" Her eyes were shining.

The King smiled at the Donkey Prince. "Will you visit here with us for a while? It would give my daughter great pleasure to hear more of your music."

"Thank you, sire," said the Donkey Prince. "If you wish it, I should like to stay."

And so the Donkey Prince stayed on at the castle. His days passed very pleasantly.

Sometimes he played with the little brothers of the Princess. He let them ride on his back, and he showed them a new game of kickball, and he taught them the names of all the trees in the wood behind the castle.

"He is so patient with them," said the nursemaids. "He is so kind!"

Sometimes he helped the King with his accounts.

"If you just move this number from here to there," he would say, "it will all come out right."

"How smart you are to straighten that out for me!" the King would say.

Sometimes he went to parties and balls.

"Isn't he charming? Isn't he gay?" the ladies would whisper behind their fans. "He has the manners of a prince!"

And the Donkey Prince spent every morning in the castle garden, talking with the Princess and playing songs for her on his lute.

"Another one! Oh, please, another one!" she would say after each song.

One day when she begged for still another one, the Donkey Prince said, "This song will be about a rose that was kissed by a princess and that turned to gold for pure joy."

As he played, the gardener stopped his work to listen, and the birds stopped fluttering about in the trees to listen, and even the flowers turned their pretty little faces toward the Donkey Prince, and listened too.

When the song ended, the Princess said, "Oh, I loved that! Now play a funny song!"

The Donkey Prince played a silly little song about a toad who tried to fly. And the gardener dropped his rake because he was laughing so hard, and a squirrel tumbled down from a pine tree, hiccuping and giggling, and the Princess laughed until the tears came to her eyes.

"Oh, play a sad one now, please do, or I shall never stop laughing!"

The Donkey Prince laughed too. "I cannot play a sad song, dear Princess," he said. "I have forgotten all the sad songs I ever knew."

And indeed, as the weeks went by, the Donkey Prince was happier than he had ever been in his life.

Then one afternoon, as he sat reading, the Donkey Prince overheard two guards talking as they walked past him.

"Really? *Three* different princes?" one was saying.

"That's right," the other guard answered. "From three different kingdoms. They have all asked to marry the Princess. And they are all such fine young men that the King can't decide which one the Princess should accept."

That night the Donkey Prince did not sleep. He walked back and forth in his room.

"She is beautiful and gentle and good," he said to himself. "Of course she will marry! She will marry a handsome prince who is straight and tall, as a prince should be!"

Just before the sun came up, he decided, "I cannot stay to see it happen. They will ask me to play my lute at the wedding, and then my heart will surely break in two."

As soon as it was daylight, the Donkey Prince went to the King and told him that he was going away.

"But we all hoped you would *never* leave us!" said the King.

"I am sorry, sire, but I feel it is time."

"Have you not been happy with us?" asked the King.

"I have been extremely happy with you," said the Donkey Prince. "Everyone here has been very kind to me. But now I truly must leave."

"The Princess will be terribly upset," said the King. "She is so fond of you."

"I am—I am fond of her, too," said the Donkey Prince. "But I cannot stay any longer."

Then the Donkey Prince went into the garden, to see the Princess for the last time.

"Good morning," said the Princess. "Do you have a new song for me today?"

The Donkey Prince could not answer her. Instead, he began to play his lute. It was a new song.

But long before he had finished it, the Princess had buried her face in her hands and burst into sobs.

"Please, please stop!" she cried. "That is the saddest song I have ever heard!"

"It is a farewell song, dear Princess," said the Donkey Prince. "I am going away."

The Princess looked up. "Away? But you cannot go away!"

"Yes, I must," said the Donkey Prince. "I know you will miss hearing my songs, but you will be able to remember them after I have gone."

"But it is not the songs I will miss," cried the Princess. "It is you!"

"You will miss *me*? Me, with my long ears and my gray fur and my tail, and such an ugly face?"

The Princess stamped her foot. "You are *not* ugly! You are just as beautiful as the music you play!"

"But I look like a donkey!"

"I don't care what you look like! I love you, and I want you to stay with me forever!"

As the Princess spoke these words, the Donkey Prince felt a sort of tickle on his chest. He looked down.

"Why, there is a button on my chest! I never saw a button on my chest before!"

The Donkey Prince touched the button with his hoof, and it unbuttoned all by itself. And then the donkey skin, head and ears and hoofs and tasseled tail and all, slid to the ground and vanished.

Instead of a donkey, there stood a fair young man, straight and tall, and dressed like a prince.

The Donkey Prince looked down at himself.

"Oh, I cannot believe it!" he exclaimed. "I look like myself at last!"

The Princess smiled. "Yes, you are very handsome indeed. But this is how I always thought of you anyway. I cannot imagine why you wore that silly donkey skin."

The Donkey Prince and the Princess decided to get married as soon as a wedding could be arranged. Then they hurried to the King.

"Father," said the Princess, "please tell the other princes that I will have none of them. Here is the man I will marry."

"What! A total stranger?" cried the King.

The Donkey Prince laughed. "I am hardly a stranger, sire. I have been living in your castle these many, many weeks."

Then the Donkey Prince and the Princess told the King what had happened.

"What splendid news," said the King. "And now you will not leave us after all!"

The Donkey Prince and the Princess were married a few days later, and the King gave them a castle of their own to live in.

As the years passed, they had six beautiful children. Three were pretty little girls with long hair, and three were handsome, bright lads. And not a single one of them was born with gray fur, or long ears, or a tail with a tassel on the end.